Bad Buster

Nobody is better at being bad than **Buster Reed** — he flicks paint, sticks chewing gum under seats and wears the same socks for weeks at a time. Of course no one wants to know him. But Buster has a secret — he would like a friend to play with.

Will he ever find one?

Happy Cat First Readers

Bad BuSter

Sofie Laguna

Illustrated by Leigh Hobbs

HAPPY CAT BOOKS

Published by
Happy Cat Books
An imprint of Catnip Publishing Ltd
Islington Business Centre
3-5 Islington High Street
London N1 9LQ

First published by Penguin Books, Australia, 2003

This edition first published 2006
1 3 5 7 9 10 8 6 4 2

Text copyright © Sofie Laguna, 2003
Illustrations copyright © Leigh Hobbs, 2003

The moral rights of the author and illustrator have been asserted

A CIP catalogue record for this book is available
from the British Library

ISBN 10: 1 905117 23 X
ISBN 13: 978 1 905117 23 9

Printed in Poland

www.catnippublishing.co.uk

For Sue, thank you for your
encouragement – *S.L.*

For Jenny, my sister – *L.H.*

1
Buster comes to Town

Nobody was better at being bad than Buster Reed.

Being bad was what Buster did best.

When Buster first came to town with his family, it didn't take long for everybody to find that out.

Buster Reed flicked paint . . .

said rude words to girls . . .

stuck chewing gum under the
seat . . . wore the same socks
every day for a month . . .

and wrote his name on the desk with a crayon.

When the teacher in class said, 'Buster Reed, do you know the answer?' Buster just poked out his tongue and said 'No!'

Buster was so busy being bad that he was having a bit of trouble making new friends. Nobody seemed to want to play with him.

Buster pretended he didn't mind being on his own. But he was only pretending. Buster minded very much. He wished he had a friend to play with.

2
A Ride on Roger's Harley

Buster's mum, Vee, was bad too.
Everyone knew she had a
big skull and crossbones tattoo
on her bum (Miranda Morell
saw it when she was getting
changed in the swimming-
pool changing rooms).

Vee Reed was *always*
late for parent–teacher
meetings. When Vee worked
in the canteen she got

everybody's orders mixed up.
It made the other mums
cross. Sometimes she gave
all the kids free ice pops

when she wasn't supposed to.

Buster's dad, Roger, was even badder than that! You could *see* all his tattoos and he never even *made* it to the parent–teacher meetings.

Roger always made a lot of noise on his motorbike when he dropped Buster off at school in the morning. Sometimes he took the car spot of the principal, Mr Meed. It made Mr Meed cross.

Roger Reed spent his time

working on his Harley and

carving sculptures out of old

tree stumps. He used a

chainsaw!

One Friday afternoon

Buster came home from
school with a letter to show
his dad. It was the third
letter from school in a week
saying he'd been *bad*.

Roger stopped work on his Harley, read the note, scratched his beard and said, 'Buster, I think it's time we found something to keep you out of trouble.'

The next morning Roger took Buster for a ride on the Harley.

3
Finding
a Friend

Soon they came to a big
brick building with a sign
over the gate. The sign said:

HOME FOR LOST AND

UNWANTED DOGS

Roger Reed rang the bell
in the office and a grey-
haired lady wearing orange
overalls and a big straw hat
came to the desk.

'Hello,' she said, 'how can I help you?'

'I'm Buster Reed,' said Buster, 'and I'm looking for something to keep me out of trouble.'

'I'm Rhonda,' said the lady, 'and it sounds like you might be looking for a dog.'

Rhonda introduced
Buster to the most lost,
most unwanted, *baddest*
bunch of dogs he had
ever seen.

Buster liked the dogs
very much.

Rhonda could see that
Buster was having a bit of
trouble deciding which one
he wanted for a friend.

'If you like,' she said to
him, 'you can come back

after school and spend
some more time with the
dogs. That might help you
to decide which one you
like the most.'

And so, on his way home from school on Monday, Buster dropped into the Dogs Home . . . and the next day after that . . . and the next day after that too. Buster and the dogs got along very well.

4
Buster and the Dogs

When Harry, the boxer, snarled at Buster, Buster just snarled right back. Soon Harry wagged his tail instead.

When Chester, the grumpy sausage dog,

turned his back on Buster,
Buster rubbed him under
his tummy and said, 'Come
on, Chester!'

Soon Chester jumped up and ran in circles whenever he saw Buster coming.

When Shirley, the three-legged poodle, snapped at Buster, Buster just snapped right back. Soon Shirley licked Buster instead.

When Lenny, the one-eyed terrier, looked too unhappy, Buster put on his unhappiest face and tickled Lenny under the chin.

It made Lenny grin and
they both felt better.

When Linda, the postman-
chasing doberman, tried to

chase Buster, he just stood
very still and looked at her.
Soon Linda began to love
chasing the sticks Buster
threw for her instead.

Buster spent lots of time
trying to train the dogs.
He took them to the park
and tried to train them to
come when he whistled.

He never had much success
but it was lots of fun
practising. Sometimes he
threw the ball for them.
They didn't bring it back
very often.

Buster had to go and get
it himself. Buster didn't
mind. The dogs made him
feel happy.

Buster liked Rhonda too.
She didn't care about his
grubby face and scabby

knees and she never
seemed to notice his smelly
socks. She was a bit smelly
herself from spending so
much time with the dogs.

Buster liked to help
Rhonda with the dogs.
Together they cleaned out
the cages . . . did lots of
washing and brushing . . .
gave the dogs food and
water . . . and took them
on big walks in the park.

Sometimes, after they'd
finished work, Rhonda took
Buster over to her cottage
next door. She showed him
all her dog books while they

ate chocolate cake and
drank tea from her best
china tea set.

Rhonda always gave
Buster as much chocolate
cake as he wanted. He
always looked very happy
when Vee and Roger came
to pick him up.

At school Buster Reed forgot to be so bad. He stopped flicking paint. He stopped saying rude words to girls. He forgot to chew gum or write his name on the desk with a crayon.

But everybody else remembered. Buster still didn't have anyone to play with.

5
Buster gets a Feeling

One Thursday afternoon,
with fifteen more minutes
of school to go, Buster got
a feeling about Rhonda
and the Dogs Home. It was
a very strong sort of quivery
feeling deep in his tummy.

The feeling told him that
Rhonda and the dogs
needed him *right now*!
Buster watched the hands
of the clock and waited for

the end-of-school bell to
ring.

At last!

Buster ran as fast as he
could. When he got to the
Dogs Home all the dogs
were barking and howling
and scratching at their
cages. He ran through the
gate to check on the dogs.

Harry was snarling.
Chester was covering his
eyes with his paws.

Shirley was snapping. Lenny
looked angry. Linda was
running round in circles.
Something was wrong.

Where was Rhonda?
Buster heard strange
bumping noises coming
from inside her house.

He ran to the front door
and knocked very loudly.
'Rhonda!' he called.
'Rhonda!'

Nobody came. Buster
decided to have a look
through the kitchen window.
He stood on tiptoe and peered
into Rhonda's kitchen. He

couldn't see anyone. Buster ran round the other side of the house. He climbed up the drain pipe and looked through Rhonda's living-room window.

There were two masked burglars in Rhonda's living room!

6
Buster and the Burglars

Buster had to think fast.
He climbed down the drain
pipe as quickly and quietly
as he could. Next he raced
round to the dogs' kennels and
opened all the gates. He was
going to need the dogs' help.

Buster ran back to the
house with the dogs
following him. The two
burglars were climbing out

of the living-room window.

They were carrying

Rhonda's television and

her best china tea set!

'Hey you! *Stop!*' shouted
Buster.

'You can't stop us, little
kid!' the burglars shouted

back, their mouths full of
Rhonda's chocolate cake.

'No,' said Buster, 'but
they can!' Buster gave his
loudest whistle, and this
time all the dogs came
running.

The burglars tried to run
away. They ran round the
back of the house. The dogs
chased them back. They ran
down the side of the house
but the dogs cut them off.

They ran down the other
side of the house and again
the dogs stopped them.

'Quick!' shouted one of
the burglars. 'Up the tree!'

The burglars climbed up the big tree in front of Rhonda's cottage.

Buster gave another big whistle. All the dogs stood around the bottom of the tree. They barked and snapped and howled up at the burglars.

The burglars were too scared to move.

7
'Good Dogs!'

Buster could hear the loud
engine noises of two big
motorbikes. It was Vee and
Roger coming to pick him up.

And, look, there was
Rhonda on the back of Vee's
motorbike! Her arms were

full of dog food from a visit
to the pet shop.

Vee and Rhonda gave
Buster a big hug.

Roger called out to the
burglars. 'Come down from
the tree!'

'We're scared of the dogs!'
they shouted back.

Buster gave one more
loud whistle. The dogs came
to Buster. They sat quietly.
'Good dogs!' he said.

'Now come down!' Roger called out again. 'The dogs won't hurt you, they do what Buster tells them!'

Buster looked very proud.

The scared burglars climbed slowly down from the tree.

'That Buster sure is good with those dogs!' said one of the burglars to the other.

8
Buster Finds Friends

The next day there was
a picture of Buster and
the dogs on the front page
of the newspaper.

**BUSTER REED
DOES GOOD**

Suddenly Buster Reed
was the school hero. For
a little while anyway.

Now sometimes Buster

Reed is good . . .

Sometimes Buster Reed

is bad . . .

And sometimes Buster
Reed is just somewhere in
between . . .

And these days Buster has
lots and lots of friends . . .
as well as one very special
friend.

From Sofie Laguna

Everyone in my family, except me, rides motorbikes just like Vee and Roger. I don't like riding them that much because I get scared I might fall off. I do like dogs though.

I have my own dog. I found him at the Lost Dogs Home. Tigger keeps the burglars away because he barks so loudly.

Most of the time Tigger and I are pretty good. Tigger's only bad when he chases people on roller blades.

From Leigh Hobbs

I've always liked dogs. And now
I have two. One is a kelpie (sheep-
dog) called Asta. She runs about
with a ball in her mouth all day, or a
rubber foot with a face on it.

Ruby, the other one, is a small Blue
Heeler, an Australian cattle dog.
Ruby eats and sleeps and
is very lazy. I had both of these
animals in mind when I drew the
pictures for *Bad Buster*.

The Princess and the Unicorn

Wendy Blaxland

No one believes in unicorns any more. Except Princess Lily, that is.
So when the king falls ill and the only thing that can cure him is
the magic of a unicorn, it's up to her to find one.
But can Lily find a magical unicorn in time?

THE LITTLEST PIRATE

SHERRYL CLARK

Nicholas Nosh is the littlest pirate in the world. He's not allowed to go to sea. 'You're too small,' said his dad. But when the fierce pirate Captain Red Beard kidnaps his family, Nicholas sets sail to rescue them!

When Anna Slept Over

Jane Godwin

Josie is Anna's best friend. Anna has played at Josie's house,
she's even stayed for dinner, but she has never slept over.
Until now…

Becky was cross with her little brother. 'If you don't leave me alone,' she said to him, 'I'll put a spell on you!' But she didn't mean to make him disappear!

Tom was given a gorilla suit for his birthday. He loved it and wore it everywhere. When mum and dad took him to the zoo he wouldn't wear his ordinary clothes. But isn't it asking for trouble to go to the zoo dressed as a gorilla?

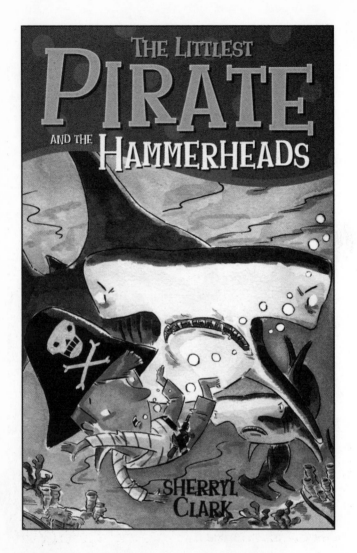

Nicholas Nosh, the littlest pirate in the world, has to rescue his family's treasure which has been stolen by Captain Hammerhead. But how can he outwit the sharks that are guarding Captain Hammerhead's ship?

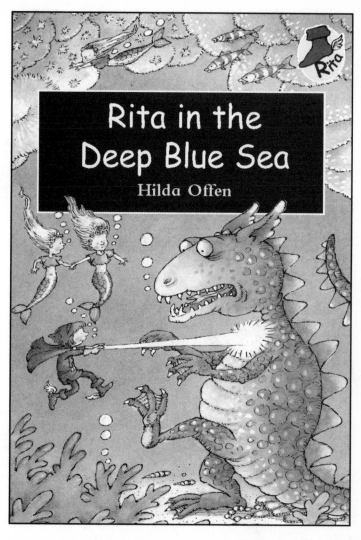

Rita's mother won't let her go on a boat with her brothers and sister. However, when she has changed into her Rescuer outfit she can ride on a turtle, tie an octopus in knots and even get the better of a mermaid-eating sea-monster!

Septimouse is the seventh son of a seventh son which makes him a truly magical mouse. Septimouse can talk to cats and humans too – he can even make them as tiny as he is. But the one thing he can't seem to do is to get his paws on some cheese!

Ann Jungman

SEPTIMOUSE BIG CHEESE!

Septimouse needs all his magical powers when little Katie's dad loses his job. But making humans mouse-sized, setting up a magnificent cheese factory –it's all in a day's work for Septimouse!

The supermouse has won the Cheese of the Year competition and
now longs for fame and fortune. If only his prize-winning cheese
recipe didn't have to be kept secret! Then disaster strikes –
only Septimouse can save the day!